MW00424580

The Magic Story

NEW EDITION
of the Inspirational Classic by

Frederick Van Rensselaer Dey

The Magic Story

UPDATED and REVISED
by STEVEN A. LAVELLE

The Magic Story: Updated and Revised

ISBN: 0-87516-801-9
Library of Congress Control Number: 2003113786
First Printing, 2004

DeVorss & Company, Publisher
P.O. Box 1389
Camarillo CA 93011-1389
w w w . d e v o r s s . c o m

Printed in the United States of America

CONTENTS

Nurture your mind with great thoughts,
for you will never be any greater than you think.

—Benjamin Disraeli

What lies behind us and what lies before us are
small matters when compared to what lies within us.

—Ralph Waldo Emerson

FOREWORD

In every generation, men and women of courage and vision have embarked on spiritual quests seeking enlightenment, meaning and self-fulfillment. With the twin candles of hope and faith they have entered invisible worlds in search of a teacher or guide who would reveal the secrets of living a life worthwhile and would place into their hands a key that would open the door to universes unimagined in their common hours. When these explorers returned, they sketched "maps" for the rest of us and sometimes, though all too rarely, these maps found their way into a public arena where anyone who cared to, could see them.

As the days turned into years and the years into decades, the maps floated along like a message in a bottle waiting for the next generation, or the next, to discover. The extraordinary book that you now hold in your hands is just such a map. It was first published over 100 years ago, and the story itself purports to have been written even *hundreds* of years before that. It first appeared in the pages of *Success Magazine* in 1900 and became an overnight sensation.

Thousands of requests for copies flooded the editor's desk until it was decided that the story should be reprinted as a small book with a silver cover. That little silver book became legend.

A character in the story confides to his friend, "I have been reading a strange story, and since reading it, I feel that my fortune is assured. Your fortune can be assured, too. All you have to do is read it. You have no idea what it will do for you. Nothing is impossible after you know this story." And similarly, a strange and wonderful thing happened. People who read the story began to circulate tales about how this little book actually did affect their lives: "I was destitute, but I read *The Magic Story* and I got an idea that made my fortune that same night!" "My company was failing until I read *The Magic Story*-then, in just 15 days, I turned everything around and now we are growing at an astronomical rate!" "My marriage was failing until I read *The Magic Story*, now my wife and I have fallen in love all over again. It truly is a magic story!"

Such accounts are undoubtedly true, but the real power of *The Magic Story* does not lie in its alleged ability to bring greater abundance into the reader's life, or to enable the reader to manifest more material wealth, or even to act as a love potion for wounded relationships.

No indeed! The real power of *The Magic Story* is far greater than that. Its true power lies in its ability to touch the spirits of those who read it and to move them to a higher realm of consciousness.

Perhaps you have heard the story of a young girl whose father tore a page from a magazine, then tore that sheet into several smaller pieces. The page had an artist's rendering of the Earth on it and the father thought that it might amuse his daughter to try and reassemble the torn pieces as one might put together a puzzle.

He left her to her task, thinking that he would have ample time to finish reading the rest of the magazine before she reappeared, but in only a few moments she returned to his side with all the oddly shaped, torn pieces perfectly taped together and the illustration totally intact.

"Sweetie!" exclaimed the surprised father, "How did you put the picture back together so quickly?"

"Oh, it was easy," she responded, "on the other side of the world was a picture of a man and a woman. So, I just put that picture together. When I got the man and woman right, all I had to do was turn the picture over and the world was right too."

And therein lies the key to the power of *The Magic Story*. It will tell you how to "... get the picture right ..." And once you have, you will know why the whole world will be within your power to "make right" as well.

Change your thoughts and you will change your life. Have a magnificent forever!

–Steven A. LaVelle

PART I

HOW THE MAGIC STORY WAS FOUND....

I was sitting alone in a cafe one day having a cup of coffee during a blustery winter storm. Outside, the weather was hideous. Snow and sleet was swirling everywhere, and the wind howled without mercy. Every time the outer door opened, a gust of unwelcome air swooped in and chilled every corner of the room. Still I was surprisingly comfortable.

The frigid weather conveyed nothing to me except an abstract thought that I was where it could not affect me. While I dreamed and sipped my coffee, the door opened and closed, and admitted -

Sturtevant, an undeniable failure. Despite his shortcomings, he was an artist of more than ordinary talent. He had, however, fallen into the rut traveled by ne'er-do-wells, and was out out of work and broke.

As I raised my eyes to Sturtevant's I became aware of a mild change in his appearance. Yet he was not dressed differently. He wore the same ragged coat in which he always appeared, and the old brown hat was the same. And yet there was something new and strange in his appearance. As he brushed the snow off his hat and shoulders, there was something new in his demeanor.

Even though I hadn't planned on dining with Sturtevant, I asked him to join me as he passed by. He nodded and sat down across from me. I asked him what he would like, and after scanning the menu carelessly, he ordered the first thing he saw then suggested I order some as well.

Thinking he would not accept, I was somewhat surprised when he agreed to sit down. This left me wondering how I would pay all the food even though I knew I hadn't enough cash to pay the bill. As I composed myself, I couldn't help but notice a spark in usually lackluster eyes, and the healthy, optimistic look in his face. I was amazed at these sudden changes.

"Have you lost a rich uncle?" I asked.

"No," he replied, calmly, "but I have found my mascot."

"Brindle, bull or terrier?" I inquired.

"Mr. Currier, my friend," said Sturtevant pausing with his coffee cup half way to his mouth, "I see that I have surprised you. I am a surprise to myself. I am a new man, a different man, and the changes took place only in the last few hours. You have seen me come into this place 'broke' many times, and even though you've turned away, so that I wouldn't think you saw me, I knew that you had. In fact, I knew why you did that. It was not because you did not want to pay for a dinner, but because you did not have the money to do it. Is that your check? Let me have it. Thank you. I haven't any money with me tonight, but I, - well, this is my treat."

He called the waiter over and, with a confident flare, signed his name on the backs of the two checks, and waved him away. After that he was silent for a moment while he looked into my eyes, smiling at the astonishment, which I in vain tried to conceal.

"Do you know an artist who possesses more talent than I?" he asked. "No. Do you happen to know anything in the line of my profession that I could not accomplish, if I applied myself to it? No. You have been a newspaper reporter for - how many - seven or eight years? Do you remember when I ever had any credit until tonight? No. Was I refused just now? You have seen for yourself. Tomorrow my new career begins. Within a month I shall have a bank account. Why? Because I have discovered the secret of success."

"Yes," he continued, when I did not reply, "my fortune is made. I have been reading a strange story, and since reading it, I feel that my fortune is assured. Your fortune can be assured, too. All you have to do is read it. You have no idea what it will do for you. Nothing is impossible after you know this story. It makes everything as plain as A, B, C. The very instant you grasp its true meaning, success is certain. This morning I was a hopeless, aimless bit of garbage on the city streets; tonight I wouldn't change places with a millionaire. That sounds foolish, but it is true. The millionaire has spent his enthusiasm; mine is all at hand."

"You amaze me," I said, wondering if he had been drinking.

"Won't you tell me the story? I must hear it."

"Certainly. I mean to tell it to the whole world. It is really remarkable that it should have been written and should remain in print so long, with never a soul to appreciate it until now. This morning I was starving. I hadn't any credit, nor a place to get a meal. I was seriously thinking about suicide.

"I had gone to three of the papers for which I had done work, and had been handed back all that I had submitted. I had to choose quickly between death by suicide and death slowly by starvation. Then I found the story and read it. You can hardly imagine the transformation. Why, my dear boy, everything changed at once, - and there you are."

"But what is the story, Sturtevant?"

"Wait; let me finish. I took those old drawings to other editors, and every one of them was accepted at once."

"Can the story do for others what it has done for you? For example, would it really help me?" I asked.

"Help you? Why not? Listen and I will tell you, although, really, you should read it. Still I will tell it as best I can. It is like this: you see, ..."

The waiter interrupted us at that moment. He informed Sturtevant that he was wanted on the telephone, and with a word of apology, the artist left the table.

Five minutes later I saw him rush out into the sleet and wind where he disappeared. Of all the cafe's regular customers, none could ever remember Sturtevant taking an urgent telephone call before. That, of itself, was substantial proof of a change in his life.

* * *

One night, on the street, I encountered a former college chum of mine named Avery, then a reporter for one of the evening papers. It was about a month after my memorable encounter with Sturtevant, which, by that time, was almost forgotten.

"Hello, old chap," he said; "how's the world using you? Still on the news desk?"

"Yes," I replied, bitterly, "with a chance of losing my job soon.

But you look as if things were coming your way. Tell me all about it."

"Things have been coming my way, actually, and it is quite remarkable, when all is said and done. You know Sturtevant, don't you? It's all due to him. I was down on my luck and feeling sorry for myself, looking for you, hoping you might lend me enough money to pay my rent, when I met Sturtevant. He told me a story. It is the most remarkable story you'll ever hear; it made a new man out of me. Within twenty-four hours I was back on my feet and haven't had a worry or any trouble since."

Avery's statement, uttered calmly, and with the air of one who had merely quoted an old adage, reminded me of the conversation I had with Sturtevant in the cafe that stormy night, nearly a month before. "It must be a remarkable story," I said, in disbelief. "Sturtevant mentioned it to me once. I have not seen him since. Where is he now?"

"He has been drawing war sketches in Cuba, at two hundred a week; he's just returned. It is a fact that everybody who has heard the story has done well since. There are Cosgrove and Phillips, - friends of mine, - you don't know them. One's a real estate agent; the other's a broker's clerk, Sturtevant told them the story, and they have experienced the same results that I have; and they are not the only ones.

"Do you know the story?" I asked. "Will you try it on me?"

"Certainly; with the greatest pleasure in the world. I would like to have it printed in big black type, and posted at every train station throughout New York. It certainly would do a lot of good, and it's as simple as A, B, C. Excuse me a minute, will you? I see Danforth over there. Back in a minute, old chap." But he didn't return and I grew tired of waiting.

If the truth be told, I was hungry. My pocket, at that moment, contained exactly five cents; just enough to pay my fare up-town, but not enough to pay for a meal. There was a "night owl" diner in the neighborhood, where I had frequently "stood up" the owner, so I went over there, and to him I applied. He was leaving as I was on the way in, and I confronted him.

"I'm broke again," I said, with extreme cordiality. "You'll have to trust me once more. Some ham and eggs, I think, will do for now." He coughed, hesitated a moment, and then walked back in with me.

"Mr. Currier is good for anything he orders," he said to the manager; "one of my old customers. This is Mr. Bryan, Mr.Currier. He will take good care of you, and ***stand for*** you, just the same as I would. The fact is, I have sold out. I've just turned over the outfit to Bryan. By the way, isn't Mr. Sturtevant a friend of yours?" I nodded.

I couldn't have spoken if I had tried. "Well," continued the ex-"night owl" man, "he came in here one night, about a month ago, and told me the most wonderful story I ever heard. Now I've just bought a place on Eighth Avenue, where I am going to run a regular restaurant-near Twenty-third Street. Come and see me." As he left the diner, the door slammed shut before I could stop him; so I ate my ham and eggs in silence, and resolved that I would hear that story before I slept. In fact, I began to wonder if I really wasn't meant to hear this story. If it had made so many fortunes, surely it should be capable of making mine.

The certainty that the wonderful story - I began to regard it as magic - was in the air, possessed me. As I started to walk homeward, rubbing the last nickel in my pocket and contemplating the certainty of riding downtown in the morning, I experienced the sensation of something secretly pursuing me, as if Fate were treading along behind me, yet never overtaking, and I was conscious that I was possessed with or by the story.

When I reached Union Square, I

searched my address book for the home of Sturtevant but it wasn't there. Then I remembered the cafe in University Place, and, although the hour was late, it occurred to me that he might be there. He was! In a far corner of the room, surrounded by a group of friends, I saw him. He discovered me at the same instant, and motioned to me to join them at the table. There was no chance for the story, however, there were half a dozen around the table, and I was the furthest removed from Sturtevant. But I kept my eyes upon him, and bided my time, determined that, when he rose to depart, I would go with him.

A silence had fallen upon the party when I took my seat. Everyone seemed to be deep in thought, and the attention was fixed upon Sturtevant. The cause was apparent. He had been telling the story. I had entered the cafe just too late to hear it. On my right, when I took my seat, was a doctor; on my left a lawyer. Facing me on the other side was a novelist that I knew. The others were artists and writers.

"It's too bad, Mr. Currier," remarked the doctor. "You should have come earlier. Sturtevant has been telling us a story. It is quite wonderful, really. I say, Sturtevant, won't you tell that story again, for the benefit of Mr. Currier?"

"Why yes. I believe that Currier has, somehow, failed to hear the magic story, although, as a matter of fact, I think he was the first one to whom I mentioned it at all. As a matter of fact, it was right here, in this cafe -- at this very table.

Do you remember what a wild night that was, Currier? Wasn't I called to the telephone, or something like that? To be sure! I remember, now; interrupted just at the point when I was beginning the story. After that, I told it to three or four people, and it ignited them, as it had me. It seems incredible that a mere story can have such a stimulating effect upon the success of so many people from such widely different occupations, but that is exactly what it has done. It is a kind of never-failing remedy, like a magic cough medicine that is guaranteed to cure everything from the common cold to back pain.

There was Parsons, for example. He is a broker, you know, and had been on the wrong side of the market for a month. He had utterly lost his grip, and was on the verge of failure. I happened to meet him at the time he was feeling the bluest, and before we parted, something brought me around to the subject of the story, and I related it to him. It had the same effect on him as it had on me, and has had on everybody who has heard it, as far as I know. I think you will all agree with me, that it is not the story itself that changes the way your mind works; instead, it is the way it is told, - in print, I mean. The author has somehow produced a psychological effect, which is indescribable. The reader is hypnotized by this mental and moral stimulant. Perhaps, Doctor, you can give some scientific explanation of the influence exerted by the story. It is a sort of elixir manufactured out of words?"

From that, the crowd started talking about the theories. Now and then slight references were made to the story itself, and they were just enough to tantalize me; the only one present who had not heard the story.

Later on, I walked around the table and seized Sturtevant by one arm, and pulled him away from the party to talk. "If you have any consideration for an old friend who is rapidly being driven mad by this story, which has an uncanny way of eluding me, you will tell it to me right now!" I said, forcefully. Sturtevant just stared at me in mild surprise.

"All right," he said. "The others will excuse me for a few moments, I think. Sit down here, and you shall have it. I found it pasted in an old scrapbook I purchased on Ann Street for three cents and there isn't a thing about it that tells you where it originally appeared, or who wrote it. When

I discovered it, I casually began to read it, and in a instant I was captivated. Before I left it, I had read it many times over, so that I could repeat it almost word for word. It affected me strangely, as if I had come in contact with a long-lost friend.

From within the story, there seems to be a personal element that applies to every one who reads it. Well, after I had read it several times, I began to think it over. I couldn't stay in the house, so I seized my coat and hat and went out. I must have walked several miles, without realizing that I was the same man, who, in only a short time before, had been in the depths of despondency. That was the day I met you here, - you remember."

At that moment they were interrupted by the waiter who handed Sturtevant a note from the front desk. It was from his employer, who urgently demanded he return back to the office. "Too bad!" said Sturtevant, rising and extending his hand. "I'm sorry to say that I must go at once. Tell you what I'll do, old chap. I'm not likely to be gone any more than an hour or two. You take my key and wait for me in my room. In the escritoire near the window you will find an old scrapbook bound in leather. It was made, I'm sure, by the author of the magic story. Wait for me in my room until I return."

I found the book without difficulty. It had a quaint, homemade feel to it, as Sturtevant had said, covered and bound with leather. The pages formed an odd combination of yellow paper, vellum and homemade parchment. And it was there that I finally found the ***Magic Story***.

PART II

INTRODUCTION

There is one great secret of success. I have experienced it, used it, and lived it. Here in my final days, I have decided to share it with the generations that follow so that they too may benefit from this truly amazing secret.

First of all, please keep in mind that I am more accustomed to using tools much heavier than a pen and since I am not a writer by trade, I need not apologize for my style of writing nor for its lack of literary merit. Even though my hand and mind are not nearly as young or nimble as they once were, I still have the clarity of thought to get to the heart of the message. Besides, does it really matter how you get the sweet nectar from the fruit? Does it matter how the orange is peeled as long as you savor what's inside?

There is no doubt that as I tell my story, I'll probably use old expressions that were popular in my youth. It seems to me that as one gets older, things of the past become clearer than things that have happened more recently; it really doesn't matter much how one expresses their thoughts as long as what results is helpful, valuable, and has real meaning with worthy intentions.

I exhausted my brain pondering the question of how to describe this recipe for success, until it became obvious that the best way to share it with you would be the same way I discovered this amazingly simple wisdom. Like all good recipes, you need good ingredients and possibly a pinch of secret seasoning or two: Likewise for the recipe for success. So for you to understand how it works, perhaps it would be best to tell you a little about the story of my life first.

Who knows? Perhaps the day will come that men and women, born generations after I am gone, will someday give thanks for the words I write.

* * *

THE MAGIC STORY

Unknown Author

My father was a seafaring man who, early in life, gave up his vocation and settled on a plantation in the colony of Virginia. Some years thereafter, I was born, in the year 1642, well over a hundred years ago. It would have been better for my father if he had listened to the wise advice of my mother by staying with the job for which he had been trained and educated, but he wouldn't listen. He blindly refused to see the good that was in his grasp. The vessel he captained was soon traded for a life on the land.

Here is the FIRST LESSON for success:

Be receptive at all times to the merit that already exists in any situation, and view each opportunity with eyes wide open. Remember that a thousand hopes for the future aren't worth a single piece of silver.

When I was only ten years old, my mother's soul took flight and two years later my worthy father followed her. I, their only child, was left alone even though there were friends who cared for me. That is to say, they offered me a home beneath their roof - which I took advantage of for five months.

There was no wealth for me from my parent's estate and as I look back over the years, I became convinced that those same friends, under whose roof I lived for a time, had defrauded both them and me.

I won't bother you with what happened to me between the ages of twelve and a half and twenty-three since it has nothing to do with this tale, but some time after, with only sixteen guineas in my pocket, ten of which I had earned myself, I took a ship to Boston. It was there that I began to work first as a cooper, repairing wooden casks, and thereafter as a ship's carpenter, but only when the ship was docked. The sea was not amongst my desires.

Fortune will sometimes smile upon an intended victim in spite of the odds being stacked against them. Such was one of my experiences. At age twenty-seven,

I was able to acquire the property where, less than four years earlier, I had worked for hire. In other words; Fortune was a part of my life long before the reality of it became apparent. I had prospered. However, Fortune is unpredictable, and she must forever be courted.

And that brings us to the SECOND LESSON for success:

Fortune is very unpredictable - it can only be retained through diligence, ingenuity and appreciation. In this, Fortune is not unlike a personal or dear friend. Treat them with neglect or disdain and they will turn their attention elsewhere.

About this time, Disaster (which is a courier of broken spirit and lost resolve) paid me a visit. Fire ravaged my yards, leaving me nothing in its blackened paths but a debt I could not pay. I approached my acquaintances, seeking assistance for a new start, but the fire that had reduced my livelihood to ash, seemed also to have consumed their sympathies. So it happened, that within a short time, not only had I lost everything, but I was also hopelessly indebted to others; and for that they cast me into prison.

It is possible that I might have rallied from my losses had it not been for this last indignity, which broke down my spirit so that I became utterly despondent. Upward of a year I was detained within the prison, and when I finally came forth, the person who emerged was not the same hopeful, happy man, who was content with his lot and full of confidence in the world and its people.

Life has many pathways, and of them by far the greater number lead downward. Some are steep, others are less so; but no matter how sharp the angle, they ultimately lead to defeat. Failure exists only in the grave. If you are alive, you have not failed.

And that is the THIRD LESSON:

You can always turn about and ascend by the same path you came down; you may even find one that is less steep (even if it takes longer to achieve), or one which is better suited to your situation, talents and abilities.

When I came forth from prison, I was penniless. I possessed nothing beyond the poor garments which covered me, and a walking stick that the prison guard allowed me to keep, since it was worthless.

However, being a skilled workman, I quickly found employment that paid good wages; but, having once eaten the fruit of worldly advantage, dissatisfaction of my humble lot possessed me. I became depressed and sullen. To cheer my spirit, and for the sake of forgetting the losses I had sustained, I passed my evenings at the tavern. Not so that I could drown my sorrow in liquor, but so that I could laugh and sing, tell jokes and have good conversations with my fellow companions.

Here you will find the FOURTH LESSON:

Seek fellowship among the industrious, for those who are idle will sap your energies from you and cause indirection.

It was my pleasure at that time to relate, upon the slightest invitation, the tale of my disasters, and to curse the men that I thought had wronged me, because it wasn't in their best interest to come to my aid. Moreover, I found childish delight in stealing from my employer, each day, a few moments of the time for which he paid me. Such a thing is less honest than downright theft.

This habit continued and grew upon me until the day dawned which found me not only without employment, but also without character, which meant that I could not hope to find work with any other employer in Boston as well.

It was then that I regarded myself a failure. My condition at the time was like a strong man who, descending the steep side of a mountain, loses his foothold. The more he slides, the faster he goes down. I have also heard this condition described by the word Ishmaelite, which I understand to be a man whose hand is against everybody, and who thinks that the hands of everyone else are against him. The Ishmaelite and the leper are the same, since both are abominations in the sight of all. Yet they differ much, for the former might be restored to perfect health. He has merely poisoned himself through grudges and imaginings, while the other has poison in his blood.

Here begins the FIFTH LESSON:

Free yourself from the harmful, self-destructive thoughts and visions you plant in your mind.

I don't mean to preach at length upon the gradual degeneration of my energies for it doesn't do anyone much good to repeatedly dwell upon misfortunes. It is enough to say that the day came where I had nothing left to purchase food and clothing with, and I found myself living like a pauper. I was occasionally lucky at times when I could earn a few coins now and then, but I couldn't find steady employment. I became emaciated in body, and naught but skeleton in spirit.

My condition, then, was deplorable; not so much for the body, but for the mental part of me, which was deathly weak. In my imagination I deemed myself ostracized by the whole world, for I had surely sunk to a miserable depth.

Here begins the SIXTH LESSON:

Your "Awakening," the final lesson, is so important that it cannot be told in just one sentence, nor in one paragraph for that matter, but must be adopted from the remainder of this tale.

I remember my "Awakening" very well, because it came in the night, when I actually did wake up from a deep sleep. My bed at the time was a pile of shavings in the rear of the cooper shop where I had once worked. My roof was the pyramid of stacked casks, underneath which I had made comfortable for myself. The night was cold and I was chilled, although, paradoxically, I had been dreaming of light and warmth. You might say, when I relate the effect this vision had on me, that my mind was oddly different in a way. So be it, for it is my hope that the minds of others might be affected likewise, which is why I have written this story for you in the first place.

It was in this dream that I met my other identity - you could call it my "double," though that does not adequately describe it. Meeting this other self of mine has somehow bestowed me with my freedom from self-imposed misery, giving me the very aid that I had in vain sought from my friends.

I remember, in my dream, struggling through a tempest of snow and wind, searching, seeking something. Through the storm by chance, I peered into a window and saw him - the other me. He was vibrant with health; before him, on the hearth, blazed a roaring fire. There was a conscious power and force in his demeanor; he was physically and mentally strong and sound.

I rapped timidly upon the door, and he insisted I come in. There was a kind, hope-filled look in his eyes as he led me to a chair by the fire, but he uttered no word of welcome. When I had warmed myself, I went back out into the tempest, burdened with the shame that the obvious contrast between us had impressed upon me. Which now brings me to the strangest part of my tale, for it was then that I suddenly awoke; only to find that I was not alone. There was now a Presence with me; intangible to others, I discovered later, but quite real to me.

The Presence was in my likeness, yet it was strikingly unlike me. The brow, not more lofty than my own, yet seemed more round and full; the eyes, clear, direct, and filled with purpose, glowed with enthusiasm and resolution; the lips, chin, - even, the whole contour of face and figure was dominant and determined.

He was calm, steadfast, and self-reliant; so different from my usual self who was cowering, filled with nervous trembling, and fearsome of unexplainable shadows. When the Presence turned away, I followed, and throughout the day I never lost sight of it, except when it disappeared for a time beyond some doorway where I dared not enter. At such places, I awaited its return with anxiety and awe, for I could not help but wonder about how the Presence (so like myself, and yet so unlike), could have the boldness and confidence to dare tread where my own feet fear to walk.

It seemed also as if on purpose, I was led to the very places and to the men where, and before whom I most previously dreaded to appear; to offices where once I had transacted business; to men with whom I had once had financial dealings. Throughout the day I pursued the Presence, and at evening saw it disappear beyond the portals tavern famous for its cheer and good living. Perhaps, in other words, I was seeking the pyramid of casks and shavings.

That night in my dreams, I did not encounter the Better Self (for that is what I have named it), but when I awakened, it was there next to me, wearing kindly, hope-filled look that could never be mistaken for pity, nor for sympathy in any form. How could this be happening to me?

The second day was not unlike the first, and I was again doomed to wait outside during the visits which the Presence paid to places where I would have gone had I possessed the necessary courage. You see, it is fear which overshadows and casts out the soul from your body, rendering it a thing to be despised. Many a time I wanted to speak to it but the words rattled around in my throat, unintelligible; and the day closed just like the one before.

This happened for many days, one following another, until I stopped counting them; strangely enough though, I discovered that constant association with the Presence was producing an effect on me. Then one night I awoke among the casks sensing that he was present and I made a bold attempt to speak, even if it was with a nervous quiver in my voice.

"Who are you?" I asked. I was startled into an upright posture by the sound of my own words; and the question seemed to amuse my companion, so I hoped there would be a friendlier tone in his voice when he responded.

"I am that I am," was the reply. "I am he whom you have been. I am he whom you may be again. Why do you hesitate? I am he whom you were, and whom you have cast out for other company. I am the man made in the image of God, who once possessed your body. Once, we dwelt within it together, as tenants in common, living and working as one. At one time, you were so selfish and petty that I could no longer abide with you, therefore I stepped out. You see, there is a "plus-entity" and "minus-entity" in every human body that is born into the world. Whichever one of these is favored by our actions, it becomes the dominant entity; that is when the other is inclined to abandon you, temporarily or forever. I am the plus-entity of yourself; you are the minus-entity. I own all things; you possess nothing. If you want me to return, I will, but this body in which we both inhabit has become unclean, and I will not dwell within it. Cleanse it, and I will gladly take possession."

"Why then, do you pursue me?" I asked of the Presence.

"You have pursued me, not I you. You can exist without me for a time, but your path leads downward, and the end is death. Now that you approach the end, you are wondering whether you should cleanse your house and invite me to re-enter. Stop what you are doing. Cleanse your mind and will of the minus-entity. Only on that condition, will I ever occupy them again."

"My mind has lost its strength," I faltered. "The will is weak. Can you repair them?"

"Listen!" said the Presence, and he towered over me while I cowered at his feet. "To the plus-entity, all things are possible. The world belongs to this side, - it is where you'll find your rightful estate. With it, you will fear nothing, dread nothing, stop at nothing. You will expect no privileges, but receive them; your requests become orders; opposition flees; you will ascend mountains, span valleys, and travel a clear and unobstructed path."

* * *

After that, I slept again. When I awoke, I seemed to be in a different world. The sun was shining and birds were soaring above my head. My body, trembling and uncertain only yesterday, had now become vigorous and filled with energy. I gazed upon the pyramid of casks in amazement that I could have lived in such a place for so long, and it was difficult to believe that I had finally spent my last night beneath its shelter.

The events of the night recurred to me, and I looked about me for the Presence. It was not visible, but sitting in a far corner of my resting place, I discovered a weak, shuddering figure, deformed of shape, looking disheveled and neglected. It tottered as it walked, for it approached me pitifully; but I laughed aloud. Some part of me knew then that it was the minus-entity, and that the plus-entity was now within me; although I did not consciously realize it then. Moreover, I was in haste to get away. There was much for me to do, and the day had just begun.

As had once been my daily habit, I turned my steps in the direction of the tavern, where formerly I had eaten my meals. I nodded cheerily as I entered, and smiled at the patrons. Men who had ignored me for months bowed graciously when I passed them on the street. I went to the washroom, and from there to the breakfast table. Afterwards, when I passed the taproom, I paused for a moment and said to the landlord, "I will occupy the same room that I once used, if by chance it's available. If not, another will do as well."

Then I went out and hurried to the old barrel maker's shop where I once worked. There was a huge wagon in the yard, and men were loading it with casks for shipment. I asked no questions, but, seizing barrels, began hurling them to the men who worked atop of the load. When this was finished, I entered the shop and found a vacant bench. It was old and worn with litter on top and looked the same as when I had worked there.

Taking off my coat, I then cleared off the old scraps, sat down to the vice-lever and started shaving barrel staves just as I had done when I worked here so long ago.

It was an hour later when the master workman entered the room, and he paused in surprise at the sight of me. There was already a hefty pile of neatly shaven staves beside me, for in those days I was an excellent workman; there was none better, but age has surely deprived me of my skill. I replied to his look of surprise with just a few simple words: "I have returned to work, sir." He nodded his head and passed on by, checking the work of other men, but from time to time he glanced over at me with a puzzled look on his face.

Here ends the SIXTH LESSON for success, although there is more to be said, since from that moment I have been a successful man, owned another shipyard, and acquired an ample supply of worldly goods.

* * *

It is of the utmost importance that you heed the following statements because your own eventual "success" depends on all that they imply:

*

Whatever you desire of good is yours. You only need to stretch forth your hand and take it.

*

Become aware of the dominant power within you that makes all things attainable.

*

Eliminate all forms of fear, for fear is the backbone of the minus-entity.

*

Apply your skills; the world must profit by them, and therefore, you.

*

Make a daily and nightly companion of your plus-entity; if you heed its advice, you cannot go wrong.

*

Remember, philosophy is an argument; the world, which is your property, is an accumulation of facts.

*

Follow your instinct and do what you are meant to do; avoid distractions that might delay your eventual success.

*

The minus-entity requests favors; the plus-entity grants them. Fortune waits upon every footstep you take.

*

Stretch out your hand, and grasp the plus-entity, which could just be waiting for you to realize and put to use.

*

Your plus-entity is beside you now; cleanse your mind, and strengthen your will. It will take possession. It waits upon you.

*

Start tonight; start now upon this new journey.

*

Be aware of which entity controls you, the other hovers at your side and could enter at any time, even for a moment.

* * *

My task is done. I have written the recipe for "success." If followed, it cannot fail. Even though I may not be entirely understood, the plus-entity of whoever reads this will fill in the gaps; and upon that Better Self of mine, I place the burden of sharing with future generations, the secret of this all-pervading goodness, - the secret of releasing and living with what is already inside of you - SUCCESS!

THE SIX LESSONS FOR SUCCESS

FIRST LESSON FOR SUCCESS:

Be receptive at all times to the merit that already exists in any situation, and view each opportunity with eyes wide open. Remember that a thousand hopes for the future aren't worth a single piece of silver.

SECOND LESSON FOR SUCCESS:

Fortune is very unpredictable - it can only be retained through diligence, ingenuity and appreciation. In this, Fortune is not unlike a personal or dear friend. Treat them with neglect or disdain and they will turn their attention elsewhere.

THIRD LESSON FOR SUCCESS:

You can always turn about and ascend by the same path you came down; you may even find one that is less steep (even if it takes longer to achieve), or one which is better suited to your situation, talents and abilities.

FOURTH LESSON
FOR SUCCESS:

Seek fellowship among the industrious, for those who are idle will sap your energies from you and cause indirection.

FIFTH LESSON
FOR SUCCESS:

Free yourself from harmful, self-destructive thoughts and visions you plant in your mind.

SIXTH LESSON FOR SUCCESS:

Your "Awakening" is within you and waiting to be discovered.